A MAGIC CIRCLE BOOK

small paul and the bully of morgan court

written by
BETTY HORVATH
illustrated by **SUSAN PERL**

THEODORE CLYMER
Senior Author, Reading 360

GINN AND COMPANY
A XEROX COMPANY

Home Office, Boston, Massachusetts 02117

Almost everyone in Paul's family was big. His mother was tall for a mother and a little bit fat. His oldest brother, Sam, was tall and strong, and his other brothers, Henry and John, were tall for their ages and still growing.

But Paul was small. He was even short for eight going-on-nine. He liked being little because there were good things about being the smallest in the family. For one thing, he always had more clothes to wear than anyone else. When Sam and Henry and John outgrew their clothes, Paul got to wear them. Right now he had a whole closetful of clothes. They weren't new clothes, but they were still good and, although some of them were too big, Paul knew he'd eventually grow into them.

Paul never minded people calling him Small Paul because his mother had said that the best things come in small packages. He knew that money and diamonds didn't take up much space and they certainly were valuable.

But then everything was different after the family moved to Morgan Court. It wasn't much fun being Small Paul anymore — and all because of the boy who lived on the corner. He was just about Paul's age, but he was big and tough-acting.

Paul met him the day his family moved to Morgan Court. He had gone for a walk around the block to see if he could find a new friend, and there right on the corner stood this big boy. Paul was about to say "Hi" when the other boy spoke first.

"You new here, kid?"

Paul nodded.

"What's your name?" he asked in a bossy voice.

"Paul. Paul Vega."

"Well, Paul, you're a regular giant, aren't you?" the big boy said and smiled an unfriendly smile.

"No," said Paul. "I'm not a giant."

"You can say that again!" said the big boy with a laugh. "Because if you're a giant, man, I'm a gorilla."

Paul wanted to say, "Maybe you're a gorilla anyway," but he thought it wouldn't be smart. So instead he said, "What's your name?"

"That's for me to know and you to find out," said the boy, pointing a finger in Paul's face. Then he spit on the sidewalk. "I live on this corner, kid, so you'd better stay out of my way. Sometimes I forget my manners." He spit on the sidewalk again.

Paul doubted that he had any manners to forget and decided that he certainly would stay out of the bully's way. But it wasn't easy. Paul had to pass that corner every morning on his way to school.

Monday, the first day of school, Paul learned that they were in the same room and that the boy's name was Willie Lopez.

Tuesday and Wednesday, Paul waited at his own doorway until he saw Willie go down the street. Then he started out, slipped safely past the corner, and ran all the way to school.

But Thursday he forgot to look, and just as he was passing the corner, he saw Willie come out of his house. Right away Willie saw Paul. "Hey, you!" he yelled. "I told you to keep away from this corner."

"Can't," said Paul. "I have to go this way to school. You know that."

"Sure I know that. But this is my corner, and every time you pass in front of my house, it's going to cost you," said Willie. "Now give me your lunch money."

"No," said Paul.

Willie knocked Paul down and took the money anyway.

6

That afternoon Paul was very hungry when he got home from school. He ate three cookies and drank a glass of milk and then took another handful of cookies.

"You'll spoil your appetite, Paul," his mother said as she put the cookie jar on the top shelf. "I've never seen you so hungry. You must be growing a lot these days."

"I sure hope so," said Paul.

He didn't tell her about the lunch money. But he thought a lot about it.

"Is something the matter, Paul?" his mother asked later.

At first Paul hesitated to tell his mother about the bully. But finally he said, "That boy who lives on the corner — Willie Lopez. I don't like him at all."

"Oh," she said. "Well, you don't have to like everybody."

"I'll never like him," said Paul. "Never!"

"Never is a long time," said his mother. "What don't you like about him?"

8

Paul was quiet for a minute.

"He's bigger than I am," he said at last.

"That's not a very good reason. I'm bigger than you are. So are your brothers. I hope you like us."

"Well," said Paul, "Willie's not just big. He's big and mean and he picks on me."

"Oh," said his mother. "That's a different story. I guess it's hard to like somebody who picks on you."

"Why does he pick on me?" Paul asked.

"Maybe because somebody picks on him," she said. "It's the old pecking order at work."

"The *picking* order?" asked Paul. "What's that?"

"The pecking order," she said. "Well, it's like this. When I was a girl, I lived on a farm and we raised chickens. Now usually the roosters seemed pretty tame, but sometimes even they had a mean day and felt like fighting. The big rooster would peck at a smaller rooster, and the smaller rooster would peck at a hen. The bigger ones picked on the smaller ones, just because it was easy to do. People are like that, too, sometimes."

"That's a good story," said Paul, "but it doesn't help me any. I'm pretty small so it looks to me as if I'll always be at the end of the pecking order."

"Well, tomorrow's another day," said his mother. "Maybe it'll be different." But it wasn't.

10

The trouble started at recess. Paul was trying to decide whether to shoot for baskets or play scatterball. He was standing on the walk minding his own business when Willie came running around the corner and bumped into him. Both boys fell down.

Willie got up and swung a fist, hitting Paul in the face. Paul was knocked to the ground again.

"You tripped me, kid!" Willie yelled.

"I did not," shouted Paul, picking himself up. "Why don't you watch where you're going, you big rooster!"

Willie approached Paul again with his fists clenched. Other children began gathering around the two boys.

"What did you call me?" Willie bellowed, looking down angrily at Paul.

Paul was angry too. He was so mad he forgot he was Small Paul talking to the bully of Morgan Court. He stood firm and looked up at Willie.

"I said you were a rooster!" he screamed.
"A big, mean, ugly rooster!"

There would have been a real fight then, but
someone spotted the teacher coming and the
crowd broke up. Willie went off mumbling
something that sounded like, "You just wait!"
and Paul knew he was in trouble. He wished
he hadn't called Willie a rooster. He wished
he were a rooster himself instead of a scared
little chicken.

Paul didn't learn very much the rest of the afternoon because he was too busy thinking about his problem. He got home from school all right by catching up with Henry and some other older boys. But there was tomorrow to think about, and the next day, and the next. The worrying he did was enough to take away his appetite.

"You're not as hungry as you were yesterday," his mother remarked.

"No," said Paul. "I'm not hungry at all."

"Do you have another problem?" she asked.

"Not another problem," said Paul. "The same old problem — Willie."

"Maybe I can help," she said.

"I doubt it," said Paul. "I've already heard about roosters and that doesn't help."

"Well there must be some way to manage Willie Lopez. You can be faster than he is, or smarter than he is, or stay away from him. Or, you can make him your friend."

"I'll never make him my friend," said Paul. "Not in a million years."

Paul dreamed that night about ten big Willies guarding the corner. They were at least eight feet tall and each one was ready to knock him down.

The next morning Paul woke up early feeling unpleasant, but he didn't know why. Then he remembered. He had to walk past Willie's house. That was enough to ruin his day.

"I wish I could stay home," he thought. "Maybe I'm sick. I think I'm sick."

"Time to get up, Paul," his mother called a few minutes later. "Breakfast is ready."

"I'm not hungry," he answered. "I think I'm sick."

"I'm making pancakes," she called back. "You're not too sick for pancakes, are you?"

"Well I guess maybe I could eat a few pancakes," said Paul, "but I don't think I'll be able to go to school."

John came over and sat on his bed. "Too bad for me you're sick," he said. "I was hoping you'd help me carry my books."

Paul almost began to feel better. "Well, if you really need me, maybe I'd better go," he decided. "And maybe you'll need somebody to carry your books after school too."

"Probably," agreed John. "That's what brothers are for." He pulled the blankets off Paul. "Time to get going or we'll be late!"

When they passed Willie's house on the way to school, they could hear a lot of yelling going on inside. It sounded like Willie was crying. John stopped to tie his shoe and listen. "What's that?"

"Sounds like the old pecking order," said Paul. "Somebody must be pecking at Willie." "Serves him right," he said to himself. "I'm glad." But it didn't make Paul feel good. It was an unhappy sound and he didn't like it — even if Willie did deserve it.

Willie was late for school. His eyes were red and watery and he kept blowing his nose.

"Do you feel all right, Willie?" Miss Baker asked.

"I have a cold," Willie muttered, and he looked unhappy. But Paul wondered.

In music class, Willie's "cold" suddenly disappeared, and he sang as usual — better than anyone else in the room. He even looked happy.

Miss Baker made an announcement. "Children, I have a surprise for you. The P.T.A. meets next Tuesday night, and they want our class to provide the entertainment. There isn't enough time to work up a play and learn speeches, but we already know a lot of good songs, so I thought we could sing for them."

Willie sat up straight and he looked eager.

Miss Baker continued. "There is one solo part in the first song. Let's vote to see who will sing it." The class chose Willie and Miss Baker nodded.

"Will you do it, Willie?"

"I guess so," Willie said, shrugging his shoulders, but he looked pleased.

"We want to have as many mothers and fathers here as possible," Miss Baker went on, "so be sure to ask your parents to come. And we will all want to look our best. Girls, wear colorful dresses. Boys, wear dark pants and a jacket."

Willie began to look unhappy again.

"Something is definitely the matter with him," Paul thought, "but it isn't any of my business. Let Willie solve his own problems. He's no friend of mine." And he walked home from school with John.

After supper Paul went out and sat on the front steps. There was nothing to do. Sam and John and Henry were off with their gang playing ball in the park. There was nobody around for Paul to play with. "If only old rooster Willie weren't rotten through and through," he thought, "I'd have a friend. But who wants to play with a bully?" He could see Willie's house from where he sat, and Willie was sitting on his steps. Then Willie got up and started walking down the street toward Paul's house.

"Oh-oh," thought Paul. "Here he comes." Paul was ready to get up and run when Willie stopped in front of him.

"This is my house," said Paul.

18

"Tell me something I don't know," said
Willie.

"Well, you'd better watch out," said Paul.
"I might forget my manners." He tried to
spit on the sidewalk, but he spit on his own
shoe instead.

"I'm not worried about you or your
manners," said Willie.

"You sure look worried about something,"
said Paul. "What were you yelling about
this morning?"

"Oh, that," said Willie. "That wasn't
anything. My old man was mad. He works
nights, and I woke him up singing. He hit
me a couple of times."

Paul thought a moment and said, "I know
what's bothering you. You're scared to sing
the solo Tuesday night."

"Me? Scared to sing?" said Willie. "Naw.
But I might be too busy to come. My folks
can't come anyhow. The old man works
and Mom has to stay home with the baby."

"Maybe you could come with us," Paul offered.

Willie looked hopeful for a minute. "Naw," he said. "I can't do it. I don't have a jacket, and I'll never be able to get one by Tuesday night. Anyhow I don't care." He sat down on the bottom step and began whistling.

Paul was thinking out loud. "You don't care and I don't care, but I bet Miss Baker cares. She thinks you sing real good."

"That's right," said Willie, "I do sing good. In fact I'm the best singer in the room — maybe even in the whole school." He whistled louder.

"Then it's too bad you don't care about Tuesday night," said Paul. "Because I know where you could get a jacket free, if you did care." Willie stopped whistling.

"Well, maybe," he said. Suddenly he yanked Paul by the collar. "Now tell me, Small Paul, where can I get a jacket?"

"From me," Paul offered. "I have a whole closetful."

Willie was ready to hit him, but he began to laugh instead. He laughed until the tears came to his eyes. "For a minute there, you had me fooled," he said at last. "I really thought you knew where I could get a jacket. You know I'm bigger than you are, Small Paul. I couldn't get into your jacket, even if I wanted to."

"I ought to give up," Paul thought. "I really ought to — even if he is the only kid my age around." "Listen, Rooster — I mean, Willie," he said. "I know I'm little. You don't have to keep reminding me. But I've got three big brothers, remember? And they're even bigger than you are. Who do you think gets the clothes they grow out of?"

Willie was listening now, and he let go of Paul's shirt.

"Probably you do."

22

"Right," said Paul. "Now do you want to borrow a jacket for Tuesday, or do you want somebody else to sing that solo?"

"Since you put it that way," said Willie, "I guess Miss Baker would sure be sorry if I didn't sing. But how come you want to lend me a jacket?"

"I don't know," said Paul. "It must be on account of your good manners."

Willie scowled at him. Then he grinned.

"You want me to teach you how to spit?" Willie asked.

Small Paul and the bully of Morgan Court sat on the steps of Paul's house and had a spitting contest until it got too dark to see.

24

BCDEFGHIJK 765432
PRINTED IN THE UNITED STATES OF AMERICA